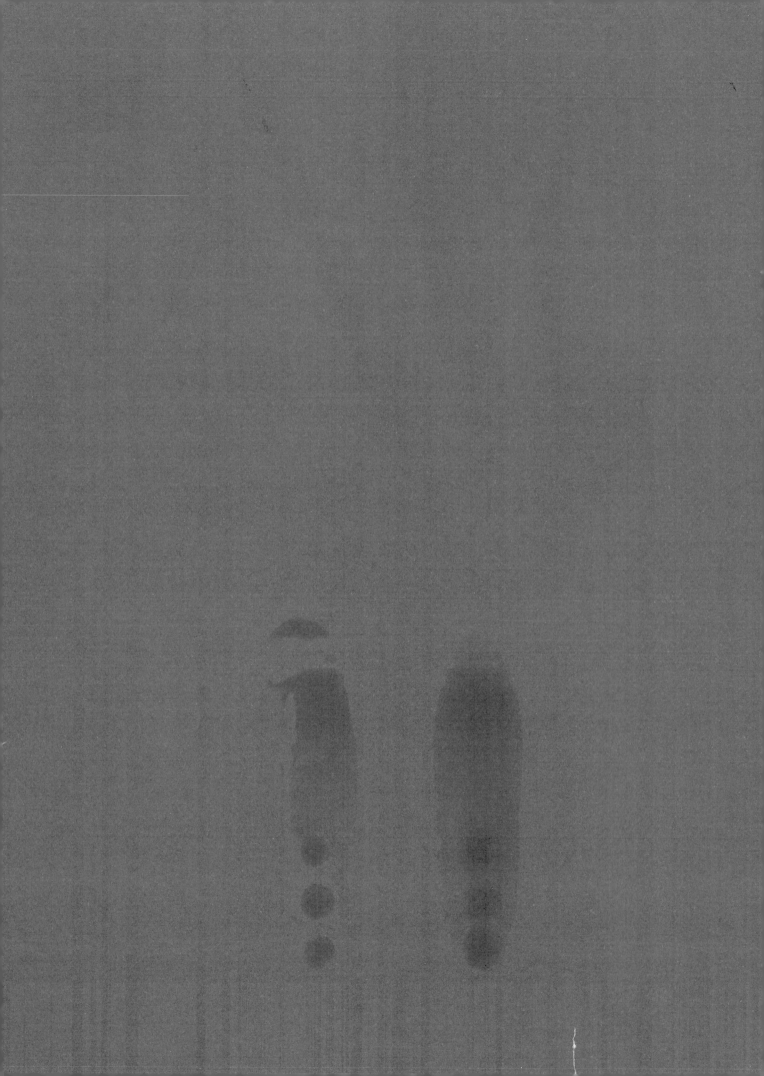

Goldilocks
AND THE
Three Martians

by
STU SMITH

illustrated by
MICHAEL GARLAND

DUTTON CHILDREN'S BOOKS ★ NEW YORK

TO MY PARENTS, BOB AND BONNIE SMITH,
FOR MAKING EVERYTHING JUST RIGHT
S.S.

TO AUNTIE ANNE
M.G.

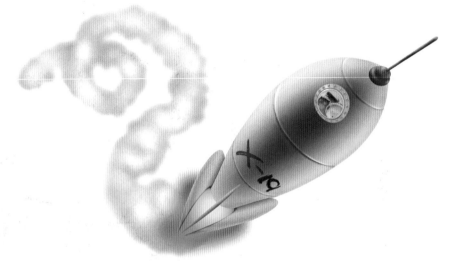

Text copyright © 2004 by Stu Smith
Illustrations copyright © 2004 by Michael Garland

Library of Congress Cataloging-in-Publication Data
Smith, Stu.
Goldilocks and the three Martians / by Stu Smith; illustrated by Michael Garland.   p. cm.
Summary: In a porridge-powered rocket ship, Goldilocks sets out to find a planet
"where everything's just right" and has a close encounter with a Martian family.
ISBN 0-525-46972-9
[1. Contentment-Fiction. 2. Space flight-Fiction. 3. Extraterrestrial beings-Fiction.
4. Characters in literature-Fiction. 5. Stories in rhyme.] I. Garland, Michael, date. II. Title.
PZ8.3.S6658Go 2004
[E]-dc21   2003049084

Published in the United States by Dutton Children's Books,
a division of Penguin Young Readers Group
345 Hudson Street, New York, New York 10014
www.penguin.com

Designed by Gloria Cheng

Manufactured in China
First Edition
1 3 5 7 9 10 8 6 4 2

Goldilocks's mom was very strict.
She gave out lots of chores.
"Please clean your room and make your bed
and straighten up those drawers."

Her mom checked homework every night.
She wasn't big on sweets—
she packed a lunch with healthy foods
like Brussels sprouts and beets.

"Wash behind your ears," Mom said.
"No eating on the couch!
Put your hat and gloves on, dear.
Stand straight and tall, don't slouch!"

Goldilocks sighed and told her pets,
"My mom is way too tough.
I'm tired of chores and homework.
That's it! I've had enough!"

So Goldilocks drew up a plan.
She had a lot to do.
It took her weeks to carry out
with screws and bolts and glue.

"Good riddance, planet Earth!" she said.
"At eight o'clock tonight,
I'm off to find a planet
where everything's *just right*!"

She filled her tank with porridge,
packed cookies just in case,
took her cat and dog along . . .

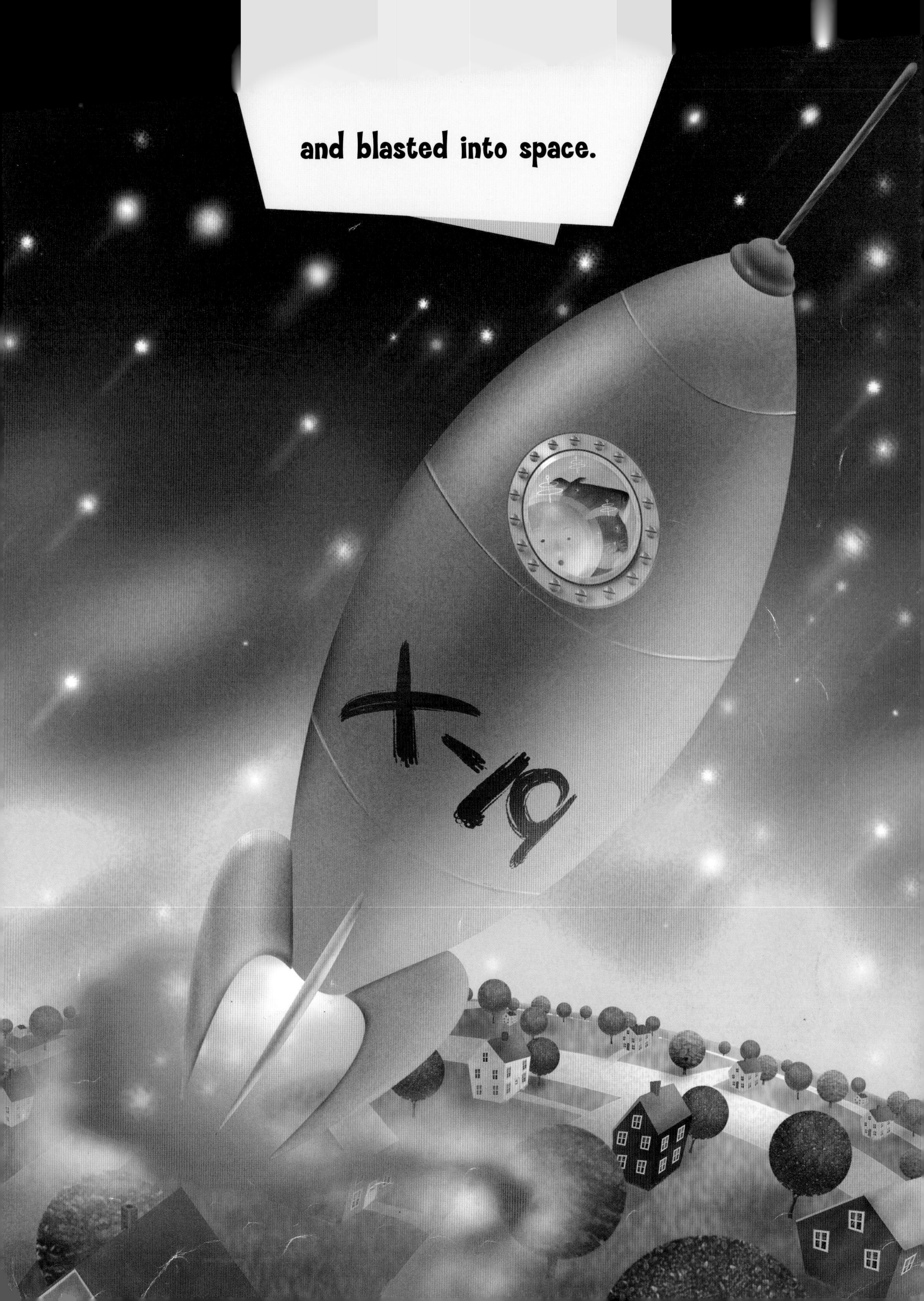

and blasted into space.

They floated round the capsule,
doing somersaults in air.
Without the pull of gravity,
they all had funny hair.

She flew to seven planets—
on each she found a flaw.
It seemed she had this problem
with everything she saw.

TOO MANY STORMS!

TOO FAR!

TOO COLD!

TOO GASSY!

"Have we been to every planet?
Let's check that map I brought.
Oops! We missed a turn back there—
here's one that we forgot!"

"Mars will be our final stop,"
she told her cat and dog
as she wrote their destination
in her handy captain's log.

After landing on the surface,
she took a look around.
"I can't believe my eyes!" she cried,
amazed by what she found.

Before her stood a Martian house.
She rang the Martian bell.
"Looks like no one's home tonight,
but what's that scrumptious smell?"

Inside she found three steaming bowls
of hearty Martian stew.
She gobbled up the smallest one
but left the other two.

"I think I'll rest my feet a while
in this comfy Martian chair."
But the first one that she sat in
sent her flying through the air.

"That chair's alive!" she screamed out loud.
"And this one's full of slime!"
But then she tried the smallest chair
and found the fit sublime.

The meal had made her sleepy,
so she headed up the stairs.
Good thing she'd thought to bring along
her trusty teddy bears.

The first bed that she sat on
was just a little high,
and as she fluffed the pillows,
one looked her in the eye.

The next bed made her seasick
(its waves were pretty steep),
but the smallest bed was cozy,
and she drifted off to sleep.

Just then the Martian family
slid in from their nightly stroll.
Before they sat to eat their meal,
Mama eyed her bowl.

"Someone's been eating my zok!" she screamed.
Papa roared, "Mine, too!"
The baby of the family squealed,
"I don't have *any* stew!"

Mama's chair spoke up to say,
"There's an *alien* in here!"
"ALIENS FOR DINNER!"
they all began to cheer.

The Martians grabbed their napkins
and slithered up the stairs.

Goldilocks was fast asleep
and dreaming of three bears.

"Something's been sleeping in my bed!"
"Something's been sleeping in mine!"
"Something's *still* sleeping in my bed!"
the baby began to whine.

Goldilocks yawned and stretched her arms,
then rubbed her sleepy eyes.
She saw the Martians ogling her
like a burger and some fries.

She popped up out of bed to leave—
their tongues were in the way!
That would have been the end of her,
but guess who saved the day?

"There goes our dinner!" Papa said.
Mama wailed, "How rude!"
The baby of the family cried,
"We *never* eat fast food!"

The trio squeezed aboard the ship.
"I think we've seen enough.
We had it pretty good on Earth—
my mom is not *that* tough!"

The Martians saw them leaving.
The baby waved good-bye.
Papa ate his napkin,
and Mama dried her eye.

Soon all three were speeding home.
They landed with a CRASH!
They woke up half the neighbors
and wound up in the trash.

"Where on *Earth* have you *been*?" Mom said.
"Why, I've been worried sick!
And what's that gizmo in the tree?
Is this some kind of trick?"

Goldilocks smiled and closed her eyes.
She held her mother tight.
"Is everything okay?" Mom asked.
"Yes, everything's *just right*."